Dedicated to the organizations and individuals who work tirelessly, ensuring voiceless animals worldwide are treated with compassion, fairness, and kindness.

- Nancy Scalabroni

"I am in favor of animal rights as well as human rights. That is the way of a whole human being."

- Abraham Lincoln

MASCOT® BOOKS

www.mascotbooks.com

For more information, please contact:
Mascot Books
560 Herndon Parkway #120
Herndon, VA 20170
info@mascotbooks.com

Library of Congress Control Number: 2014959440

CPSIA Code: PRT0115A
ISBN-13: 978-1-63177-020-3

Printed in the United States

CougaMongaMingaMan
Meets Maggie

Nancy Scalabroni

illustrated by Terri Kelleher

Maggie

CougaMongaMingaMan's tail had healed nicely from the snakebite, although in place of fur, there was now a bare spot.

The hot days of summer had passed and Couga,
along with his friends, Miss Pittypat, Snow, Tonto,
and Two-Face, continued to meet in the shady park.

Two new cats, Niki and Tilly, had moved into the neighborhood and quickly joined Couga and the rest of the group. The seven felines passed the days eating, playing, and sleeping.

Since the snakebite incident, the company of cats often heard Couga's humans calling him. "Cou-gaa, come home. Come on, Cougie." This continued until CougaMonga gave up and started home.

"It's not worth resisting," Couga told his friends.

"So long as I get fed whenever I ask, I don't need humans pawing over me," said Tonto, watching Couga walk away.

"We know how much you like attention," replied Niki.

"Yeah, as much as I like a flea collar," retorted Tonto, swatting at a falling leaf.

Everyone in the group, in particular Niki, knew Tonto didn't mean half of what he said. Recently, while climbing a tall tree, Niki had seen Tonto through a window, curled next to his humans.

One day, after being called home, CougaMongaMingaMan rushed back to the group, his tail twitching furiously.

"My humans brought home a DOG!" he told his friends.

"What?" said the group in unison. Well, all except Tilly, who just yawned.

Couga continued, "They called me home to introduce me to my new *sister*!"

"Well, the nerve of including us in the same cat-agory as a dog!" said Niki, rolling on his back.

"You should mutiny!" said Tonto, who loved giving advice. "Leave a dead lizard on the bed, break a favorite vase, scratch up…"

"What nonsense, Tonto!" interrupted Miss Pittypat.
"Dogs are very interesting creatures."

"Why not give her a chance, Cougie?" suggested Snow,
who was busy grooming her tail.

"It's not that I dislike dogs," said Couga, "I just wish my humans had warned me."

"I think you might be worried your sister will receive all the attention," said Miss Pittypat, eyeing a squirrel.

It was true. Up to this point, Couga had been, "King of the House." Now, he would have to share his humans.

The cats agreed that Couga should invite
his new sister-dog to their group.

The following day, CougaMongaMingaMan
showed up alone.

"My humans won't let her outside," said Couga,
jumping up to join Snow on the fountain. "She has
to be on a leash or stay inside the fenced backyard."

"Precisely why they are inferior," said Tonto.

Snow stopped drinking from the fountain and said, "In that case, we'll go visit her." The group walked to the back of CougaMonga's house and up to the fence. Tonto, Niki, and Couga made a clean jump over, while Two-Face, Snow, Tilly, and Miss Pittypat slipped underneath.

The surprised cats came face-to-face with Maggie as she came running toward them. Tonto, Snow, and Tilly arched their backs, while Two-Face and Niki ran up the nearest tree. Miss Pittypat had her claws out when Tilly exclaimed, "Don't worry! She's wagging her tail!"

"I don't see a tail!" cried Two-Face from the tree.

The dog came to a halt in front of the cautious cats and stood staring at each of them.

"Hi, Maggie, these are my friends," said CougaMongaMingaMan. Maggie stood wagging her stubby tail, not sure of what to do next.

"Don't even think of chasing us,"
warned Miss Pittypat.

Suddenly, Maggie lowered her head to the same level as her front feet and raised her tail end into the air. "What's she doing?" asked Tilly.

"I think she wants to play," said Couga.

Maggie charged CougaMongaMingaMan, who ran to the top of a picnic table, while the rest of the group scattered.

"I said I don't want to be chased!" cried Miss Pittypat, scrambling up the tree to join Two-Face and Niki.

Within a short time, Maggie grew tired of the game where she was the only one chasing. She stopped suddenly and paused to drink from her water bowl.

"Great. Now she's going to drool," said Tonto.

CougaMongaMingaMan jumped down from the picnic table and walked toward his sister-dog.

"I think you'll be okay with a little training," said CougaMonga, sitting down in front of Maggie. The group watched as Couga was covered with wet dog kisses.

"Yikes!" said Tonto.

CougaMonga's humans came outside and were amazed to see so many animals in their backyard. The lady held a bowl of food in her hand, which she placed on the ground. "Cougie, you've been so nice to your new sister, everyone deserves a treat."

CougaMonga felt proud of his humans and new sister. All his doubts about being pushed aside because of Maggie disappeared.

That same evening, Niki climbed to the top of a large oak tree in CougaMonga's yard. As he peered into the living room, he saw Couga's humans relaxing in their chairs.

Close by, inside the new dog bed, curled the very contented CougaMongaMingaMan and Maggie.

About the Author

Nancy's love for animals has translated into a delightful series based on one of her companion cats. Her first book in the series, *CougaMongaMingaMan…The cat with the very long name and the very long tail*, was the recipient of several book awards. They include: Purple Dragonfly Winner, Finalist in the National Indie Excellence Awards and Silver Winner from the Literary Classics Book Awards. In addition, the illustrator, Terri Kelleher, was awarded the Kuykendall Image Award from Cat World Association for her vivid and expressive illustrations.

In the second book of the series, *CougaMongaMingaMan Meets Maggie*, the author introduces several more real-life companion animals she has cherished. Nancy lives in Palos Verdes, California and is busy working on the third Couga installment of the series.